MARY-KATE & ASHLEY

Starring in

OUR LIPS ARE SEALED™

Novelization by Eliza Willard

Based on the teleplay by
Elizabeth Kruger and Craig Shapiro

HarperEntertainment
An Imprint of HarperCollins*Publishers*

A PARACHUTE PRESS BOOK

PARACHUTE PRESS

Parachute Publishing, L.L.C.
156 Fifth Avenue
New York, NY 10010

DUALSTAR PUBLICATIONS

Dualstar Publications
c/o Thorne and Company
1801 Century Park East
Los Angeles, CA 90067

HarperEntertainment

An Imprint of HarperCollins *Publishers*
10 East 53rd Street, New York, NY 10022.

For information, address HarperCollins Publishers Inc.,
10 East 53rd Street, New York, NY 10022.

ISBN 0-06-106665-6

HarperCollins®, ■®, and HarperEntertainment™ are trademarks of
HarperCollins Publishers Inc.

First printing: January 2001

Printed in the United States of America

outta site!
mary-kateandashley.com
Register Now

Visit HarperEntertainment on the World Wide Web at
www.harpercollins.com

10 9 8 7 6 5 4 3 2 1

CHAPTER ONE

Mary-Kate Parker burst out of her house, her blue eyes hidden behind her sunglasses. Her sister, Ashley, wore exactly the same shades. They walked confidently down the street, perfectly in sync.

Mary-Kate slid her sunglasses up on top of her head. Ashley did the same. Their blond hair shone in the sunlight.

"First day of high school," Mary-Kate said, glancing at her sister.

"Hope we'll be popular," Ashley added.

They flipped their sunglasses down at exactly the same moment. Turning the corner, they strode down the sidewalk toward the high school building. Kids milled about outside the building, waiting for the first day of school to begin.

A hush fell over the crowd as Mary-Kate and Ashley walked by.

"Hey, it's the Parker sisters!" one girl whispered.

"Their hair is so cool," another girl said, sighing.

"Their clothes are so hip," a third girl said.

The first girl ran after Mary-Kate and Ashley, shouting, "Can we be more like you?"

The other girls clamored after them. "You're the most popular girls in school!" one shouted.

"You're the most popular girls of all time!" another cried.

Mary-Kate and Ashley smiled coolly as they started up the steps of the school building. The principal was waiting for them at the top.

"Today has been declared Parker Sisters Day!" he announced. And with that a huge banner unfurled in front of the school. On it was a gigantic blown-up picture of Mary-Kate and Ashley.

The girls turned and waved to the cheering crowd. Confetti sprinkled the school like snow as the students cheered and called out the sisters' names. Two skywriting jets wrote WELCOME TO HIGH SCHOOL, MARY-KATE AND ASHLEY in puffy white letters against the pale blue sky. Mary-Kate sighed with contentment as the school bell rang....

Mary-Kate sat up with a start. She stared at the pastel bedroom walls around her, wondering for a moment where she was. Then she reached over and slapped the alarm clock until it stopped ringing.

The curtain beside her bed drew back with a

swish. Ashley sat up in her bed on the other side. The sisters shared a tiny bedroom but had put up a curtain between their beds. That way each girl could pretend to have her own room.

"Great dream," Mary-Kate said wistfully.

"Wasn't it?" Ashley sighed.

Mary-Kate thought it was cool to share dreams with her sister. It happened pretty often. After all, they were twins. But just then she had something more important on her mind.

It's the first day of high school, Mary-Kate thought as she eyed Ashley. *The most important day of my life.*

I've got to get into the bathroom first!

Each girl smiled at the other as they inched ever so slightly toward the edge of their beds.

Suddenly, both girls made a dash for the bathroom. They reached the door at exactly the same time—and got stuck in the doorway.

"Come on, Ashley," Mary-Kate protested. "I called it last night." She pushed against her sister, trying to get past her. But Ashley pushed back.

"I called it last Thursday," Ashley said. "Would you please move? I'm stuck here!"

"So am I!" Mary-Kate said, giving another push. Then she had an idea. "Hey, look, there's Brad Pitt!"

she cried, pointing over Ashley's shoulder.

"Where?" Ashley spun around. Mary-Kate slipped into the bathroom, slamming the door in Ashley's face. Hah! Score!

Stuck outside, Ashley glared at the closed door. "Hey!" she cried.

But Mary-Kate didn't answer. All Ashley heard was the sound of water hitting the side of the shower stall.

Ashley wandered down a short, narrow hall into a tidy kitchen. In their dream, she and Mary-Kate lived in a beautiful, spacious, modern house. But in real life, they lived in a tiny trailer home.

Ashley found her mother, Teri, talking on the phone while she scrambled some eggs.

"I can't tell you, Joan," Ashley's mother was saying. "I promised Tina I wouldn't tell anyone where her husband went."

Ashley poured herself a glass of orange juice. Her mother backed up to grab a plate, bumping into Ashley.

"Okay, I'll give you a hint," Teri said into the phone. "It's a place surrounded by uniformed guards and they have bars in every room." She listened for a minute. "No, *not* the Holiday Inn."

Ashley kissed her mother on the cheek. As she

4

sat down to drink her juice, she noticed smoke coming out of the toaster oven. She sighed. Nothing new there. Her mother burned the toast practically every day.

"Mom—the toast!" she called.

Her mother glanced at the smoking toaster oven. "Got to go, Joan," she said into the phone. She quickly hung up and flipped open the toaster oven. The toast was on fire. With a knife she tossed it toward the sink.

Ashley's father, Rick, happened to step into the kitchen at that very moment. He caught the burning piece of toast, blew out the flame, and took a bite.

"Just the way I like it," he mumbled, his mouth full of charred bread. Black crumbs scattered over his blue uniform.

He swallowed his bite. "Well, another day walking the streets," he said, reaching for his jacket.

"I hate to think of you out there alone every day, unprotected...." Teri said, putting her arms around him.

Ashley smiled. Her parents were so cute together!

"That's the life of us men in uniform," Rick replied. "You knew that when you signed on to this marriage, Teri." He kissed her, then bent down to give Ashley a kiss on the cheek.

"But it's so dangerous," Teri protested.

"You're telling me," Rick said. "Bunch of animals out there on those streets." He saluted his wife and daughter and stepped out the door to begin his rounds.

"I hope you're proud of your father, Ashley," her mother said. "Not every girl is lucky enough to have a father who's a mailman."

"Uh-huh," Ashley replied, not really paying attention. Outside the trailer, she could hear dogs barking.

"Your poor father," Teri muttered. "Those animals are after him again!"

Ashley got up and headed back down the narrow hall just as Mary-Kate stepped out of the bathroom with a towel wrapped around her head. "All yours," she said to Ashley.

Ashley took a quick shower. She was blow-drying her hair when Mary-Kate barged in with *her* hair dryer.

"I can't see the mirror," Mary-Kate complained, elbowing Ashley. She turned on her dryer. It blew Ashley's hair.

"Watch it!" Ashley cried. She blew her dryer on Mary-Kate's hair, making it stand straight up.

"Hey!" Mary-Kate protested. She aimed her hair

dryer at Ashley on purpose. Ashley turned her dryer on high and shot back. In moments, both of their 'dos were ruined.

Suddenly, the lights went out. "Oh, no!" Mary-Kate whispered. "We blew a fuse!"

"Girls!" their mother called from the kitchen. "Hurry up! You're going to be late for cheerleading tryouts!"

"What are we going to do?" Ashley wailed in the darkness. "It's the first day of school, it's time for cheerleading tryouts—and I can't fix my hair! I can't even see it in the mirror!"

"What else can we do?" Mary-Kate said. "We'll have to go as we are."

They waved good-bye to their mother and burst out of the trailer. "High school, here we come!" Ashley said.

CHAPTER TWO

The head cheerleader was a sixteen-year-old junior named Vanessa. She lined up all the freshman girls who wanted to be cheerleaders. Mary-Kate and Ashley stood at the end of the line. Their hair was a mess. This felt nothing like the first day of school they'd experienced in their dreams.

We want to be popular, Mary-Kate said to herself. She bit her lip. *But I don't really see that happening.*

Vanessa marched up and down the line, studying the girls. Her friends, the other cheerleaders, followed her every step. "Kind of a scrawny crop this year," she grumbled. She stopped when she saw Mary-Kate and Ashley. She stared at their messy hair in disgust.

"Girls, Halloween isn't until October," she sniffed. Her friends giggled.

"Then why are you acting like such a witch?" Ashley snapped.

Mary-Kate's breath caught in her throat. A hush fell over the crowd. Mary-Kate elbowed Ashley in the ribs. Was she totally insane?

Vanessa glared at Ashley. "You're going to pay for that—whoever you are," she snarled.

A few minutes later Mary-Kate and Ashley found themselves in a human pyramid—at the bottom.

"You had to open your big mouth," Mary-Kate grumbled.

"It just slipped out!" Ashley whispered to her. "Besides, you know I'm a blabbermouth. We both are. It's the family curse!"

"Shhh!" Mary-Kate hissed. "You're not supposed to talk about that!"

Mary-Kate grimaced as Vanessa stepped on her, climbing up the pyramid. She stood proudly at the top, her arms outstretched. "Go, Cougars!" she shouted.

"Somebody's been cheating on her diet," Ashley muttered, straining to hold up the weight of the girls on top of her.

Mary-Kate's nose twitched. She wiggled her nose, trying to hold back a sneeze.

But when a sneeze wants to come out, nothing can hold it back.

"Uh-oh," she groaned.

"No!" Ashley cried. "Don't do it!"

"Ah-choo!" Mary-Kate sneezed. She braced herself for disaster.

Nothing happened. Whew! She glanced at Ashley.

"That was close," Ashley said. "Wait—here's a tissue."

To Mary-Kate's horror, Ashley lifted one hand off the ground and reached into her pocket.

"Ashley, no!" Mary-Kate cried. "Put your hand back down!"

But it was too late. The pyramid toppled like a bunch of human bowling pins. Mary-Kate cringed when she saw Vanessa hit the ground.

After that it got *really* ugly. The paramedics came. They put Vanessa on a stretcher and began carrying it to the ambulance. As she passed Mary-Kate and Ashley, she shook her fist and mumbled something.

Mary-Kate could tell Vanessa wasn't seriously hurt—she was shouting too loudly. But Mary-Kate couldn't understand what she was saying, since Vanessa's jaw was wired shut.

Ashley turned to her sister. "Does this mean we didn't make the squad?" she asked.

"Our first day of high school, and our reputations are already trashed," Mary-Kate complained as she and Ashley walked home that afternoon. "How are we ever supposed to show our faces again?"

"You worry too much," Ashley said. "Everything will be fine. Trust me—by tomorrow, nobody will even remember what happened."

They turned a corner. Down the street, Mary-Kate glimpsed a mob of girls standing around, yelling and waving their arms. She squinted. Those outfits looked awfully familiar....

"Aren't those cheerleaders from our school?" Ashley asked.

Then someone in the crowd spotted them. "Hey—there they are!" one girl shouted, shaking her pom-poms. "The girls who ruined the pyramid and made Vanessa fall!"

"Let's get them!" another girl shouted.

The mob of cheerleaders thundered toward Mary-Kate and Ashley. The girls took one look at each other. "Run!" they both yelled.

Mary-Kate and Ashley raced down the street. The mob chased after them, getting closer and closer.

Mary-Kate glanced over her shoulder. "They're gaining on us!" she cried. "Quick! Into this grocery store!"

Mary-Kate and Ashley ducked into the small store.

A few seconds later the mob of angry cheerleaders ran past.

"Whew! That was close," said Ashley.

"Yeah," Mary-Kate agreed. "But as soon as we go out that door, they'll find us." She glanced around the store. "We need a disguise."

"I've got an idea," Ashley said.

Mary-Kate looked at her sister skeptically. She knew all about Ashley's great ideas.

A little later the girls left the grocery store. They walked quickly down the street with brown paper bags over their heads. Ashley had cut holes in each bag for their eyes. Both girls wore their sunglasses over the eye holes.

Mary-Kate nervously glanced around. She hoped the mob was long gone by then.

"I told you this would work," Ashley said proudly.

"Okay, but eventually they'll figure out who we are," Mary-Kate pointed out. "I mean, how many paper-bag heads are there in this town?"

"Don't worry," Ashley assured her. "By the time they figure it out, we'll have a Plan B."

Just ahead, a man was selling hot dogs from a street cart. "All this running has made me hungry," Ashley said.

"Me, too," Mary-Kate agreed.

Ashley pushed her paper bag up on top of her head. "Two hot dogs, please," she said to the man.

While the man prepared the hot dogs, Mary-Kate took off her paper bag. Then she glanced behind her. They were standing in front of a museum. Over the entrance hung a hugh banner that read ON DISPLAY INSIDE: THE FAMOUS KNEEL DIAMOND FROM THE KING TUT COLLECTION.

The Kneel Diamond? Mary-Kate thought. She nudged Ashley. "Have you ever heard of the Kneel Diamond?"

Ashley shook her head. "Never."

"Hmph." Mary-Kate crossed her arms over her chest. "Then I guess it's not so famous after all."

The hot dog vendor handed them their hot dogs. Mary-Kate slathered hers in mustard while Ashley struggled with the ketchup bottle. The top seemed to be clogged.

"I'm having a bad condiment day," Ashley complained.

"Give me that," said Mary-Kate. She snatched the ketchup bottle out of Ashley's hand. Out of the corner of her eye, she saw two men dressed in tight black suits with black masks over their faces. They were hurrying out of the museum.

As they ran out, a deafening alarm went off.

Startled, Mary-Kate squeezed the ketchup bottle hard.

"Whoops!" she said.

Ketchup jetted out of the red plastic bottle. It shot through the air and landed with a *splat* on one of the masked men. At the same moment, a black sedan screeched to a halt and backfired with a *bang!*

"I'm hit!" the masked man cried. He collapsed at Mary-Kate's feet. The other masked man jumped into the black car. The car raced away, tires squealing.

Mary-Kate and Ashley stared at the unconscious man on the ground. What was wrong with him?

"Dude, are you okay?" Mary-Kate asked. Feeling a little nervous, she bent down and pulled off his mask.

At the sight of his face, both girls gasped and took a step back.

"Look at that zit!" Mary-Kate cried.

The man had a giant pimple on one cheek. A really big, gross one.

"No wonder he's wearing a mask," Ashley said. She shuddered.

Three police cars sped up, their sirens wailing. The man on the ground suddenly came to life.

Mary-Kate thought she saw him drop something inside Ashley's backpack. But she forgot all about that as the police jumped out of their cars and hurried toward her and Ashley.

Hey! she thought, startled. They looked pretty mad!

Panicked, Mary-Kate and Ashley threw their hands up into the air.

"If—if this is about the cheerleading pyramid..." Ashley began.

"It was an accident!" Mary-Kate cried.

The police didn't speak to the girls. They grabbed the man in black and dragged him to his feet.

"She just sneezed!" Ashley went on.

The police put handcuffs on the man in black.

"And one thing led to another..." Mary-Kate added. She was getting tired of holding her arms up in the air. But she didn't dare put them down.

The officers hauled the man over to a police car and put him inside, slamming the door shut. Then they got in and drove away, leaving Mary-Kate and Ashley still standing beside the hot dog cart with their hands up.

Mary-Kate stared after the police car. *They completely ignored us!* she thought. *What just happened?*

She turned to Ashley. "You know how some days

are just like any old day?" she asked. "And other days change your life forever? I think today might be one of those days."

"Which kind?" Ashley asked. "The kind that's just like any old day? Or the kind that changes your life forever?"

"The kind that changes your life forever," Mary-Kate replied.

"Oh," Ashley said. She thought about that for a second. Then she asked, "Do you think we can put our hands down now?"

CHAPTER THREE

The next thing they knew Mary-Kate and Ashley found themselves in a courtroom. It turned out that the famous Kneel Diamond had been stolen from the museum while Mary-Kate and Ashley were buying their hot dogs. Now they were witnesses for the prosecution. The masked man who had fainted at their feet was accused of the crime—even though the diamond had never been found. No one knew where it was.

Ashley sat on the witness stand. Mary-Kate and their parents watched from the gallery. The masked man sat at the defense table with his own lawyer, glaring at Ashley. *He sure looks like he's having a bad day,* she thought.

A thin, blond woman lawyer questioned Ashley about the masked man.

"Did this man have any distinguishing features?" the lawyer asked.

Ashley made a face. "If you call a majorly gross zit distinguished," she replied.

"Would you recognize that gross zit"—the lawyer stopped to correct herself—"I mean, *blemish*, if you saw it, miss?"

"Definitely!" Ashley declared.

The lawyer addressed the judge. "Your Honor, I'd like to introduce as Exhibit Ten the following photograph.".

She pressed a button and a slide was projected onto a screen at the front of the courtroom. The slide showed the face of the masked man. His pimple was clearly visible.

The lawyer pressed the button again. The slide changed. This time it was a close-up of the huge pimple.

Everyone in the courtroom gasped in disgust. Ashley saw Mary-Kate covering her eyes with her hands. She couldn't blame her sister. What a total gross-out!

"Is this the blemish you saw?" the lawyer asked Ashley.

Ashley swallowed hard. "Yes," she answered bravely. "That's the one."

The masked man protested to the judge. "Your Honor, I was under a lot of stress that day!"

The judge pounded his gavel. "I've heard enough!" he said. "For the crime of stealing the

Kneel Diamond, which has yet to be recovered, I hereby sentence you to twenty years in prison!"

The crowd in the courtroom gasped again. The masked man leaped to his feet. "No!" he shouted. Two policemen grabbed him and dragged him away. Mary-Kate and Ashley waved politely to him as he passed by.

Ashley stepped down from the witness stand and joined her family. "Well," she said with a sigh of contentment. "That's a happy ending, right?"

"Wrong," said Mary-Kate. She looked worried. "I have bad news. While I watched you give your testimony, I couldn't help overhearing those two guys talking." She pointed to a chubby young man and a smooth-faced older man with slicked-back hair. They were sitting in the row in front of the Parkers.

"So?" Ashley replied.

"So that young goon helped Mr. Zitface steal the diamond—only the police never caught him."

Ashley stared at Mary-Kate. "How do you know?"

Mary-Kate shrugged. "I heard him say so. Anyway, the older goon is his uncle, Emil Hatchew."

"Bless you," Ashley said.

Mary-Kate rolled her eyes. "It wasn't a sneeze. It's his name. Hatchew. He's the head of the notorious Hatchew crime family, from the little-known nation of"—she paused, frowning in concentration—"Yurugli!"

"Hey!" Ashley protested. "If I'm ugly, then *you're* ugly, too. We're sisters, remember?"

Mary-Kate sighed. "It's the name of the country. Yurugli—it's somewhere in Europe, Ashley."

Ashley glared suspiciously at Mary-Kate. "Well— okay."

Emil Hatchew suddenly jumped up from his seat. He turned toward the two girls and jabbed a finger at them. Mary-Kate's heart skipped a beat.

"You girls will pay for this!" Hatchew cried.

A hush fell over the courtroom.

"Nobody crosses Emil Hatchew!" he added.

Everyone in the courtroom immediately cried out, "God bless you!"

Emil Hatchew turned to the gallery. "Like that's the first time I've heard *that* one," he said bitterly.

Then he turned back to the girls. "I'll hunt you down like a dog hunts bones," he threatened. Two big goons, obviously relatives of his, came up behind him and dragged him away. "Like a squirrel hunts nuts!" Hatchew raved. "Like a goldfish hunts those little flakes at the top of the water!"

Mary-Kate and Ashley stared after him as the goons pulled him out of the courtroom. Everyone else in the room stared at Mary-Kate and Ashley. Mary-Kate glanced at her parents, whose mouths hung open in terror.

Then Ashley rolled her eyes. "That guy," she sniffed. "What a drama queen."

"Uh, I think he was kind of serious," Mary-Kate said.

Ashley blinked. "Oh, no," she said. "He couldn't have meant all those things he said."

She paused. Her face began to turn pale. "Could he?"

CHAPTER FOUR

"Mr. and Mrs. Parker, the FBI is concerned about the safety of your family." A very serious man named Agent Banner had called the Parkers into his office after word reached him of Emil Hatchew's threats. Agent Banner was middle-aged and looked kind of nervous. With him was a younger investigator named Agent Norm.

"Until Emil Hatchew is permanently behind bars," Agent Banner said, "your lives are in danger."

Ashley reached over and clutched Mary-Kate's hand. She couldn't believe it. Was that horrible man really going to hunt them down like a goldfish hunts those little flakes at the top of the bowl?

Agent Norm slapped a folder onto the table. "I've reviewed your file. And in my expert opinion I've determined that—"

Ashley caught Agent Banner shooting a nasty look at Agent Norm.

"—uh, Agent Banner will take over from here," Agent Norm said, picking up the folder.

"Tomorrow you will be placed in the Witness Protection Program. It's a program the FBI uses to safeguard people who testify against dangerous criminals," Agent Banner explained. "You will be moved to a new city and receive new identities. No one will know your whereabouts except for Agent Norm and myself. That includes your friends—and your family."

"Everyone?" Teri Parker protested. "But my half sister's stepbrother is going through a terrible divorce...."

"I'm sorry, Mrs. Parker," Agent Banner said. "That includes everyone." He turned to Rick Parker and added, "And, Mr. Parker—I'm afraid you'll have to give up your job as a mailman."

Rick swallowed hard. A few tears welled up in his eyes.

Mary-Kate heaved a deep sigh. "Poor Dad."

"Girls," Agent Banner said. "I have bad news for you, too. Unfortunately, you'll have to go a new school."

The girls glanced at each other. Was this really, actually happening to them?

"You mean...we can never go back to our old school?" Mary-Kate asked. She sounded as if she were afraid to believe it.

Agent Banner shook his head.

Ashley felt like jumping for joy. *We're saved!* she thought. *We never have to face that angry mob of cheerleaders again! We can start over at a new school. Maybe this time we won't be losers from day one.*

"I'm sorry, girls," Agent Banner was saying. "That's just the way it has to be."

"Gee, what a shame," Mary-Kate said. Ashley could tell she was struggling not to smile.

"Oh, well. Bring on those new IDs!" Ashley said.

"Not so fast," Agent Norm cut in. "If for any reason your cover is blown, we'll have to relocate you immediately. In other words—keep your mouths shut."

Now the girls exchanged worried looks. Keeping their mouths shut would be easier said than done.

"We can't do that!" Ashley protested. "Mom told us our family history. For generations, we have been known as blabbermouths!"

Oops. Ashley quickly covered her mouth. Her mother had told her not to tell anybody. But how could she help it?

Being a blabbermouth ran in her family!

CHAPTER FIVE

It started off well enough. The Parkers quickly packed up and moved to Texas. Their new home was a small but cute house with a picket fence around it.

"Nice house," Mary-Kate said as the movers hauled the boxes inside.

"A lot nicer than our old trailer," Ashley said. "This Witness Protection Program is okay with me."

"I wonder what kids wear around here," Mary-Kate said as they walked inside.

"This is Texas," Ashley replied. She waved a hand. "Everyone in Texas dresses like a cowboy. Even the girls."

Mary-Kate shrugged. "Makes sense," she said.

But when they showed up for school the next day in their cowboy boots and cowboy hats, they were shocked to see that no one else was dressed that way. Their classmates wore the same kind of clothes the kids in California wore.

Mary-Kate felt like crawling into her brand-new

locker and staying there. "Off to another great start," she whispered as the teacher led her and Ashley to their desks.

"Class, we have two new students with us today," the teacher announced. "Carla and Andrea Frauenfelder. Why don't you girls tell us about yourselves? Stand up, Carla."

Mary-Kate and Ashley both stood up at the same time.

"*I'm* Carla," Ashley whispered to Mary-Kate.

"No, *I'm* Carla," Mary-Kate insisted. "You're Andrea."

Ashley thought for a second. "Oh. You might be right," she whispered. Then she pointed to Mary-Kate and said to the whole class, "She's Carla."

Mary-Kate rolled her eyes. The kids were staring at them as if they'd just landed from outer space.

"Carla?" the teacher prompted.

"Uh—what was the question again?" Mary-Kate asked.

"What brings you two to Texas?" the teacher repeated.

"Oh, right," Mary-Kate said. "Well, we witnessed a crime."

"And now we're in hiding," Ashley piped up.

The teacher and the class gasped. Mary-Kate

clapped her hand over her mouth. Ashley thunked herself on the forehead.

The next day the movers came back, loaded up the truck, and drove the Parker family away. They returned to Agent Banner's office. Agent Banner seemed very annoyed with them.

"Sorry," Ashley apologized. "It just slipped out." She shrugged and smiled, hoping Agent Banner wouldn't yell at her.

"I'm sure it won't happen again," her mother said.

Agent Norm pushed a pile of folders across the table toward the Parkers. "Here are your new identities," he told them.

Ashley couldn't help noticing that Agent Banner's eye was twitching slightly. *He's kind of a touchy guy,* she thought.

The Parkers moved to Seattle. Mary-Kate and Ashley dressed for school in their most fashionable grunge wear—big plaid workshirts, jeans, and knit caps. They made friends right away.

They'd been in Seattle for just a couple of days when a group of kids invited them out to a coffee bar after school. Ashley gazed around happily. *This is great!* she thought.

"I can't wait for the homecoming dance!" Mary-

Kate said as she sipped a double decaf mochaccino.

"The band is going to be so cool," said one of their new friends. "Just watch out for the slammers."

"Hey," Ashley blurted out. "We just sent some jewel thieves to the slammer!"

Her new friend's jaw dropped. Mary-Kate rolled her eyes. Ashley put her hand to her mouth. "Oops," she said.

The movers arrived that afternoon to take their stuff away. The Parker family found themselves at the FBI office again.

Agents Banner and Norm looked even more irritated this time. Mary-Kate cringed slightly as Agent Norm gave them the folders containing their new identities.

"Third time's a charm, right, guys?" Rick Parker said.

The girls smiled sheepishly.

The Parkers were flown to Pennsylvania Dutch country. Their third day there, Mary-Kate and Ashley were invited to a quilting bee. They put on the clothes they were given to wear—long brown dresses and stiff white bonnets.

"It's kind of like being in a play about the

Pilgrims or something," Ashley said, trying to be cheerful.

Mary-Kate's shoulder blades itched from the scratchy wool as the girls walked into the quilting bee. Mary-Kate gazed around in horror. A dozen women sat in a circle, sewing. They all wore drab brown dresses just like Mary-Kate's and Ashley's.

No, no, no, Mary-Kate thought. *This just isn't going to work!*

She glanced at Ashley. Ashley gave her a nod.

Mary-Kate walked to the middle of the circle. "Excuse me, everybody," she said loudly. "We're in the Witness Protection Program!"

She smiled at Ashley. That ought to do it!

Agent Banner's eye twitched a little more furiously as he gave the Parkers their next identities. Ashley couldn't stop watching it. *He looks as if he's about to lose it,* she thought. *I wonder why he's so tense?*

The Parkers moved to Miami next, then Chicago, New York, Wichita, Albuquerque, Boston, St. Louis, Minneapolis, Indianapolis, Annapolis, Saginaw, Ho-Ho-Kus, Tallahassee....

"There's always Hawaii, right?" Ashley suggested when they found themselves at the FBI headquarters for the hundredth time that month.

"No, there isn't," her dad said in an irritated voice. "We've already been there."

Agent Norm scowled. Teri Parker sighed wearily. "Hey, what happened to that nice Agent Banner?" she asked.

"Uh," Agent Norm said a little nervously. "Agent Banner is taking some—uh, some time off."

"That eye twitch got out of hand, right?" Ashley suggested.

"In a way," Agent Norm replied. He cleared his throat. "At any rate, people, I'm in charge now." He stood up, puffed out his chest, and strutted back and forth across the office. "You people have left me no choice," he went on in a booming voice. "We're sending you to the last place on the planet. A place so remote, so clever, that no one would *ever* think of looking for you there...."

"Oh, I know!" Ashley cried. "Australia!"

Agent Norm looked shocked. "How on earth did you know?"

Mary-Kate raised her eyebrows. "Uh, dude?" She pointed to the big map on the wall. Australia was circled three times in red, with red arrows pointing to it.

Agent Norm shook his head. "Oh," he said. Then he cleared his throat again. "Anyway, if you screw it up this time, you'll be pulled from the program. Permanently."

As they left the office, Mary-Kate grabbed her sister's hand.

"This is our last chance," Mary-Kate told Ashley in a serious voice. "This time we have to make it work—for Mom's and Dad's safety! And for our own."

"I know," Ashley said. She shook her head, worried. "But what if we don't like Australia?"

"Tough," Mary-Kate said. "This time we'll have to stick it out—no matter what."

CHAPTER SIX

"Wow!" Ashley gasped as she stood on the porch. She gazed at the view in awe. Their new house in Sydney, Australia, overlooked a harbor near the famous Manley Beach. Mary-Kate and Ashley couldn't believe that all this—the beautiful blue ocean, the clean white sand, all the people sunning and playing volleyball and surfing—all this lay practically in their own backyard.

"This is like one big party!" Ashley cried.

"The trouble is—we haven't exactly been invited yet," Mary-Kate said.

The girls were still getting used to their new identities: Abby and Maddie Turtleby from Cleveland, Ohio. Rick and Teri Parker were now Shirley and Stanley Turtleby, owners of the Surfside Inn, a bed-and-breakfast overlooking the harbor. Mary-Kate and Ashley—otherwise known as Maddie and Abby—couldn't believe how cool their new life was.

The inn's staff included Katie Smith, a beautiful,

brown-haired twenty-eight-year-old who was in charge of scuba diving, wind surfing, and sailing. Shelby Shaw, a grizzled, tough, cigar-smoking old man, ran the inn's fishing boat. He could catch a fish with his bare hands. The inn even had its own mascot—a kangaroo named Boomer.

Mary-Kate and Ashley settled into life at the inn quickly. On their first night, Boomer let Mary-Kate give him a pedicure.

"School's tomorrow," Mary-Kate said as she dipped her nailbrush into a bottle of polish. The girls were relaxing in their cozy new bedroom. "It's a chance for a fresh start."

"We should probably skip cheerleading tryouts," Ashley suggested.

"Good plan," Mary-Kate agreed. "What do you think we should wear?"

"Don't worry," Ashley assured her. "I've got the whole Aussie fashion thing under control."

The next morning, the girls showed up at school dressed for the Australian outback. They wore khaki shorts, matching khaki shirts, kneesocks, and outback hats.

As they walked down the hall, Mary-Kate couldn't help noticing that no one else was wearing an outback hat. Or khaki shorts. Or kneesocks.

They were dressed in cool modern clothes. A couple of kids pointed at them and laughed.

"This is your idea of 'under control'?" Mary-Kate complained.

"Look at the bright side," said Ashley. "At least they speak English."

A tall, freckle-faced girl approached Mary-Kate and Ashley and smiled. "Welcome to Steak and Kidney," she said. "What's with the barro daggy duds? You seppos gone troppo?"

Huh? Mary-Kate glanced at Ashley, worried. Ashley was nodding and smiling. But Mary-Kate was pretty sure her sister hadn't understood a word this girl said, either.

The girl offered her hand. "The name's Sheila."

"I'm Abby," Ashley said. "And this is Maddie."

"What brings you Sheilas to our end of the world?" Sheila asked.

"Oh," Ashley said, preparing to tell everything. "We're in the—"

"—mood to see the school," Mary-Kate interrupted. She wasn't about to let Ashley spoil everything this time. "Would you mind showing us around?"

Sheila led them to the schoolyard. Kids were hanging out, listening to music. Sheila pointed out a good-looking girl who was laughing with her good-looking friends.

"That's Victoria," Sheila explained. "And the popular crowd."

Mary-Kate and Ashley perked up. The popular crowd?

"Forget them," Sheila warned. "They'll never talk to you."

Mary-Kate and Ashley slumped, their hopes dashed.

Next Sheila pointed out a group of cool-looking kids wearing T-shirts and surf shorts.

"That's Pete and Avery and the surfies," she said. "Don't talk to them if you want to be popular."

"But you just said the popular kids won't talk to us," Mary-Kate protested, puzzled.

"Right," Sheila said. "But on the off chance they might, I'd stay clear."

One of the surfie boys, tall, tan, and blond, walked by. Pete, Mary-Kate remembered. He caught Mary-Kate's eye and winked. Mary-Kate quickly looked away, but she couldn't help thinking that he was pretty cute, surfie or not.

Sheila pointed out a group of awkward, goofy-looking kids and said, "Those are the nerds. They'll be friends with you even if you barf all over them."

She waved and called out to a red-haired boy with buckteeth. "Hi, Leonard!"

Leonard waved back. Then he tripped and fell on his face.

"Which group are you in, Sheila?" Ashley asked.

"I'm in the individualists," Sheila said proudly. She pointed to a group of girls who looked exactly like her—tall and freckle-faced with pigtails.

Mary-Kate and Ashley smiled politely. But inside Mary-Kate's heart sank. The popular kids wouldn't like them—especially if they hung out with the surfies. They didn't want to be nerds. And they didn't fit in with the individualists.

It's hopeless, Mary-Kate thought. *We've been all around the world, and no matter where we go, we never fit in.*

Will we ever fit in anywhere?

CHAPTER SEVEN

"What's the point, Katie?" Mary-Kate said with defeat in her voice. She and Ashley were standing on the dock next to Katie's motorboat, watching Katie coil ropes. "We're never going to fit in here."

Katie had just opened her mouth to speak when Shelby Shaw emerged from the cabin of his fishing boat.

"Couldn't help overhearing," he said, taking a sip from a can. "And I think I can help. Girls, take it from Shelby Shaw. You want to make friends here in Steak and Kidney, this is what you do."

He threw back his head, finishing his drink in one gulp. Then he took the empty can and smashed it against his forehead until it was nothing but a flat circle of tin.

Mary-Kate's jaw dropped. Ashley raised her eyebrows skeptically.

"*That's* going to make us popular?" Ashley asked.

Shelby shrugged. "Goes over big at the Shark Hunter's bake-off. I'm the most popular guy there!"

The girls frowned. Shark hunters were *not* the kind of people they were trying to impress.

Ashley shook her head and turned back to Katie.

"Girls," Katie said, "you want to fit in with the Aussies? Here's my secret."

The girls leaned closer, eager to hear Katie's advice.

"Stop worrying!" Katie said. "And have fun. Why don't you go to the beach?"

Disappointed, the girls headed inside to change into their bathing suits. A few minutes later they were sitting on the beach, watching a gourmet chef barbecue shrimp and fish for Victoria and her friends.

Ashley sighed. "Are we having fun yet?"

"No," Mary-Kate admitted. "But *they* are."

Donnie and Ray, two of Victoria's friends, were tossing a boomerang. Victoria lounged on her designer towel, laughing.

"Ray, toss me another prawn, will you?" she asked.

"Anything for you, Vic," Ray replied. He plucked a plump, juicy prawn off the grill and handed it to Victoria.

Mary-Kate's mouth watered as she watched Victoria gobble up the giant shrimp. She glanced down at her own cheese sandwich and sighed. *It's not much,* she told herself. *But it's better than nothing.*

She took a bite of her sandwich. Something gritty crunched against her teeth. She spit out the bite and opened her sandwich. It was covered with sand.

She glanced across the beach at Victoria. Victoria picked up her towel to shake it out. "Look!" she cried, bending over to pick up something off the sand. "A hundred-dollar bill!"

Ashley gasped. She picked up the corner of her beach towel just in case something valuable was hidden under it. "Ugh!" she groaned. "A melting cherry Popsicle."

Behind them, the girls heard someone shouting, "G'day, Maddie! G'day, Abby!"

At least Maddie and Abby have a friend, Ashley thought. *Whoever they are.* She watched Donnie and Ray throwing the boomerang. They looked so...popular.

Someone tapped her on the shoulder. She turned around to find Sheila frowning at her and Mary-Kate.

"Hello!" Sheila said. "Earth to Sheilas!"

"Ohhh. Right," Mary-Kate said. She kicked Ashley's leg. "Maddie and Abby."

"That's us," Ashley said, bonking herself on the forehead. "Duh."

"I want you to meet my gal pals," Sheila told them. She gestured toward three of her look-alike friends. "This here's Sheila," Sheila said, pointing to the first girl. "And this is Sheila," Sheila continued. The second girl waved.

"And this here's—" Sheila began, but the third girl interrupted her.

"Erica," the third girl said. "But my friends call me Sheila."

Ashley smiled. At least it would be easy to remember their names!

"You Sheilas want to join us over there?" Sheila number one asked, pointing in the direction of a bunch of nerds. "There's plenty of room."

Ashley watched as Leonard opened a can of soda. The soda sprayed everywhere. His friends ducked. "Leonard!" they all groaned.

"Uh, what's wrong with your friend Leonard?" Ashley asked Sheila.

"Nothing," Sheila replied. "Why?"

Ashley cringed as she watched the soda can nearly slip out of Leonard's hands. He tried to hang on to it, bouncing the can like a hot potato. His friends cleared out of his way.

"Actually," Sheila whispered, "he's more than a friend."

"Ohhhh," Ashley said, nodding.

"But please, *please* don't tell anyone," Sheila begged. "I don't want Vic and her posse giving me the raw prawn over it."

"Hey," Mary-Kate said, gesturing toward Victoria. "Do you think you could...introduce us?"

The Sheilas stared at them with open mouths. "Are you a few sheep short of a station?" Sheila number one asked. "Those girls wouldn't talk to any of us if we were the last Sheilas on earth."

"And that's fair dinkum," added Sheila number four.

"Heads up!" Donnie suddenly yelled. A second later the boomerang landed on Mary-Kate's towel. She picked it up and absentmindedly tossed it back.

The boomerang sailed through the air—and returned to Mary-Kate's hand like a homing pigeon.

Donnie ran up, breathless. "Uh, your Frisbee's broken," Mary-Kate told him. She tried to toss the boomerang to him, but it returned to her again. She caught it perfectly.

Donnie's eyes widened. "Where'd you learn to 'rang like that?" he asked.

"I, uh..." Mary-Kate stammered.

Ashley threw her arm around her sister and came to her rescue. "She's the boomerang champ of Chicago."

"Cleveland," Mary-Kate corrected her.

"Whatever," Ashley said.

Victoria and her friends suddenly surrounded Mary-Kate and Ashley.

"Hi," Mary-Kate said to them. "I'm Millie."

"Maddie," Ashley corrected her sister.

Mary-Kate shrugged. "Whatever."

Victoria stepped forward. "'Whatever'? Is that a big saying with you Americans?"

"Well, *cool* Americans," Ashley explained.

Ray, dark-haired and muscular, smiled at Ashley. "We're just heading out for a surf," he said, pointing toward the water. "Want to give it a go?"

Ashley shaded her eyes as she looked at the surfers riding huge waves. She swallowed hard. *Yikes,* she thought. *That looks dangerous!*

But she let Ray lead her to the water. Soon she found herself bobbing in the ocean on a surfboard, waves crashing around her.

"Arms extended," Ray instructed her. "Slide forward." Ashley did as he told her. "That's it," he said. "Curl your fingers round the board. Then jump up."

Ashley curled her fingers around the board all

right—until her knuckles were white. "Jump up?" she cried. "When?"

"Now!" Ray shouted.

"Now?" Ashley asked. Stand up on the surfboard? Was he crazy?

"Now!" Ray repeated.

Here goes nothing! Ashley thought. She jumped up on her board.

Back on the beach, Donnie pointed toward the surf and cried, "Hey, Maddie—isn't that your sister?"

Mary-Kate turned around and saw Ashley riding a wave like a pro. Her jaw dropped. Who knew Ashley could surf?

Victoria scowled. "Since when did *she* learn to surf?"

"Since right now, I guess," Mary-Kate said. She still couldn't believe it.

"She's a natural!" Donnie said.

From that moment on, Mary-Kate and Ashley began to pick up Australian ways. Every day they fit in more and more with their new friends. Only Victoria refused to accept them.

"Boring," said Victoria.

Both girls learned how to talk like real Australians.

"So I put on me jumper and hoed into some

tucker. But me breckie had chook and snags," Mary-Kate said.

"We don't like to whinge, but we said bring on some damper and hot chockie," Ashley added.

Victoria's friends laughed, then turned to Victoria to see if she approved.

"So-so," Victoria said with a sniff.

Mary-Kate was getting worried. Unless Victoria accepted them, they couldn't be in the popular group. But what else could they do to impress her?

Then Mary-Kate had an idea. It was their last chance for coolness.

She and Ashley gathered Victoria and her posse around them on the beach.

Mary-Kate handed Ashley an empty soda can. She had one for herself, too. "Ready?" she asked.

"Ready." Ashley grinned.

"One, two, three!" Each of them smashed her soda can against her forehead.

There was a moment of silence. Mary-Kate and Ashley both looked anxiously at Victoria. What did she think?

And then—

She smiled and gave them the thumbs-up.

Mary-Kate and Ashley jumped up and down. They were in with the popular crowd!

CHAPTER EIGHT

"Hey, Maddie! Abby!"

Mary-Kate and Ashley were walking down the beach with Ray, Donnie, Victoria, and her girl-friends, when Sheila called out to them from her blanket. She was with Leonard and the other Sheilas. Leonard was eating a big sandwich.

Mary-Kate and Ashley waved to them. But Donnie said, "Look who it is! Leonard the spaz boy."

As if on cue, Leonard's sandwich fell apart all over him. In a second, he was covered in lettuce, mayonnaise, and roast beef. He gazed sadly down at himself.

Victoria and her friends laughed at him as they walked by. Victoria leaned close to Ashley and whispered, "I can't believe Sheila's really friends with that dag."

"Actually, they're more than friends," Ashley confided. Then she quickly covered her mouth. *What have I done?* she thought. *Sheila made me promise not to tell! Oh, I'm such a blabbermouth!*

Victoria grinned. "You mean they're doing the lip mash?"

"Victoria, don't tell anyone," Ashley pleaded. Victoria only laughed.

"Hey, get this, everyone!" she called—and repeated exactly what Ashley had told her.

"Kiss, kiss!" Donnie made smooching noises at Sheila and Leonard. Sheila stared at Ashley in shock. The shock quickly changed to an angry, hurt look.

Oh, no, Ashley thought, her heart sinking. She and Mary-Kate exchanged guilty glances.

Just then, Pete, the cute surfie who had winked at Mary-Kate on their first day, strolled past. He was with another guy who was equally cute. The two boys carried their boards toward the water.

Ray and Donnie elbowed each other. Then they stepped forward and blocked the surfies' path.

"And just where do you surfies think you're going?" Victoria demanded.

"This is *our* beach," Donnie declared.

"Is someone talking to us, Pete?" the taller surfie boy asked, gazing over Donnie's head.

"Nobody that I can see, Avery," Pete replied.

"Well, you better listen," Ray threatened. "Or there's going to be trouble."

"Ray, you've been watching way too much *Baywatch*," Avery drawled.

Ashley let out a giggle. Victoria and her friends shot her a nasty look.

"Look, we just want to surf," Pete said calmly. "Why don't you bludgers go back to looking in the mirror, or whatever it is you do for a living."

Mary-Kate couldn't help admiring Pete and Avery as they headed off toward the water. They weren't afraid to stand up to anybody. She looked at Donnie and Ray again, standing there, trying to look tough.

Somehow, they didn't seem so cute anymore.

Victoria must have noticed that both Ashley and Mary-Kate were a little intrigued by the surfies. She stepped between the sisters. "Girls, I'm having a party on my dad's yacht this Friday," she said. "I'd love for you to come."

"Great!" Ashley said.

"Cool!" Mary-Kate added. She was psyched. Victoria's father's yacht was huge and very fancy.

"But…" Victoria added. "In case I forgot to lay out the rules of the game…hang out with Pete and Avery and you can forget about the party. You can forget about hanging out with me and my friends, too."

Mary-Kate wanted to glare at Victoria. But she

didn't dare. She just lowered her gaze meekly.

Victoria stalked away to start a volleyball game. Mary-Kate and Ashley gazed out to the water, watching Pete and Avery surf.

"They sure are cute," Mary-Kate murmured.

"Uh-huh," Ashley agreed.

She didn't say anything else. But Mary-Kate knew Ashley was thinking the same thing she was: *Is it worth giving up being popular to be with them?*

CHAPTER NINE

Everything was going so well, the girls almost forgot why they were in Australia in the first place—to hide from Emil Hatchew.

"Girls, we have some guests joining us for dinner tonight," Mrs. Parker announced as Mary-Kate and Ashley returned from the beach.

"Our first guests!" Mary-Kate said.

"Business is picking up! Way to go, Mom!" Ashley added.

Her mother smiled. Ashley knew she'd been bored in Australia with no friends to talk to and nothing to do. Maybe having a few guests around would make her feel better.

The girls went to their room to change for dinner. When they stepped into the dining room, they found their parents and Shelby talking to two strange-looking men. The younger, skinnier one looked to be in his mid-twenties, with spiky dark hair, a goatee, and an earring in his right ear. The older man was in his fifties. He was big and bulky, with large, muscular arms and a beefy, scowling face.

"I don't like the looks of either one of them," Ashley whispered to Mary-Kate.

"Girls, I'd like you to meet Mac and Sidney," Mr. Parker said. Mac was the young one and Sidney was the older one. "These are my daughters, Abby and Maddie."

"Abby and Maddie?" Mac seemed surprised. "But I thought their names were—"

Ashley saw Sidney kick Mac under the table. Mac winced and shut his mouth with a snap.

The girls sat down at the table.

"So, Mac and Sidney," Rick said. "Are you here for business or pleasure?"

"Business," Sidney said at the same moment as Mac said, "Pleasure."

"For us, business is a pleasure," Sidney said.

"We're travel agents, touring beautiful Austria," Mac explained.

"Don't you mean Australia?" Ashley asked.

"Exactly," Mac replied.

Ashley glanced at Mary-Kate. Who were these guys? Something about them wasn't right.

Ashley picked up a casserole dish, then set it back down, wincing. It had a shark fin sticking out of it.

"Uh, Mom?" she asked. She couldn't believe what her mother tried to get them to eat sometimes.

"It's shark casserole," her mother explained. "Shelby gave me the recipe."

"The secret ingredient is a pinch of whale blubber," Shelby said through a mouthful of chewed-up shark. Ashley lost her appetite just watching him.

"What about you folks?" Mac asked. "Where are you from?"

The Parkers answered all at once.

"Texas," said Mom.

"Delaware," said Dad.

"Maine," said Ashley.

"Oregon," said Mary-Kate.

They all looked at one another. Ashley sighed as she realized none of them had said what they were supposed to say—Cleveland.

"We've moved a lot," Dad explained.

Katie Smith rushed into the dining room. "Sorry I'm late," she said. "Scuba lesson ran long." She paused and added, "I didn't know we had guests."

Mary-Kate kicked Ashley under the table and nodded toward Mac. He was staring at Katie as if she were the most beautiful woman he'd ever seen.

"Hi," Katie said to Mac and Sidney. "I'm Katie,

the water-sports instructor. You need any special attention, just whistle."

Mac let out a low, pathetic whistle as Katie sat down and began to eat.

"Mmmm—shark casserole," she said, smacking her lips. "My favorite!"

"Is that new?" Mary-Kate asked Ashley. She pointed at Ashley's necklace. It was a big, sparkling rock attached to a pink ribbon. It was the next morning, and the girls were out window-shopping.

"I found it in my backpack," Ashley replied. "It must have fallen out of my jewelry-making kit. What do you think?"

Mary-Kate studied the necklace, then wrinkled up her nose. "Kind of nineties," she said, dismissing it. She stared at a sequined dress in a shop window.

"What do you wear to a yacht party?" Ashley asked. "An inflatable dress?"

But Mary-Kate didn't seem to hear her. She was staring absentmindedly through the window.

"Hello?" Ashley nudged her sister. "Pulse check?"

Mary-Kate blinked. "Sorry. I was just thinking.... There's something weird about those travel-agent guys that we had dinner with last night."

"Duh," Ashley said. "They like shark casserole."

"No, I mean, we haven't had any guests since we got here. Suddenly, these two goons show up—" She paused to look Ashley in the eye. "You haven't...blabbed about us to anyone, have you?"

Ashley gasped. "You're accusing *me* of blabbing? What about you?"

Mary-Kate started walking briskly down the street. "I didn't," she promised.

"Well, I didn't, either," Ashley insisted.

"Are you sure?" Mary-Kate pressed.

"I can't believe you!" Ashley huffed.

They were so busy arguing, they didn't watch where they were going. They turned a corner—and bumped right into Pete and Avery.

"Hey!" Pete cried. "Nice bumping into you."

"Sorry," Ashley said. She began to tug on Mary-Kate's sleeve. "Come on, Maddie."

"Wait!" Avery said. "We were just heading over to the amusement park—"

Mary-Kate jumped in. "That sounds really cool. We'd love to go!"

Ashley stared at her sister. What was she doing? She tugged on Mary-Kate's sleeve again and said, "But we can't. We've got, um, stuff to do."

Avery raised an eyebrow. "You mean Victoria

might not like it if you come with us."

"That's not what I said," Ashley protested. Her cheeks began to heat up.

"It's what you meant," Avery said.

Pete turned to Mary-Kate. "Do you do everything Victoria tells you to?" he asked her.

Mary-Kate looked at Ashley.

He's right, Ashley thought. *Why are we letting Victoria tell us what to do?*

"Let's go!" Ashley cried.

They followed the boys down the boardwalk to an amusement park. The gates to the park were locked.

"It's closed," Ashley said.

Avery grinned. "Not for us." He pulled a key out of his pocket and unlocked the gate.

"Avery's dad owns the place," Pete explained.

"Wow!" Mary-Kate exclaimed. They stepped inside the empty park.

"It's a little creepy without anyone around," Ashley admitted.

"But that's a good thing," Avery said. "No lines! Which ride do you want to try first?"

"The roller coaster!" Mary-Kate and Ashley said at once.

With Avery at the controls, Pete and the girls

rode the roller coaster until they couldn't stand it any longer.

"Now the Ferris wheel!" Ashley exclaimed the minute she stepped off the roller coaster.

Pete and Mary-Kate ran the Ferris wheel while Ashley and Avery took a ride. Ashley loved the view from the peak of the Ferris wheel. She could see all along the coast of Sydney.

Down on the ground, Mary-Kate found herself chattering away to Pete as the Ferris wheel went around and around. He was so easy to talk to! She hadn't felt this comfortable with a guy in a long time.

"So what brought your family to Sydney?" Pete asked her.

"We...I..." Mary-Kate struggled not to blab. She wished she could tell Pete the truth—he seemed like such a nice guy. But it was too dangerous.

"My parents inherited the inn," she finally said.

"Really? From who?" Pete asked.

Mary-Kate racked her brain, trying to think of an answer. "Um...they inherited it from...some dead guy."

Pete gave her a funny look. *Oh, boy,* Mary-Kate thought, her heart sinking. *That sounded dumb.*

She soon forgot about it, though. She was

having too much fun riding the bumper cars, the wonder wheel, and—one more time—the roller coaster.

Pete and Avery are great guys, she thought. *Why can't we hang with them* and *be popular? It's not fair!*

CHAPTER TEN

"Come on, Dad," Mary-Kate said. "It's your anniversary!"

Mary-Kate and Ashley had noticed that their parents didn't seem to be having as much fun in Australia as they were. Rick and Teri were bored at the inn with only two guests. So Mary-Kate had an idea—to send them on a camping trip to celebrate their anniversary.

"It's out of the question," their dad said. He reached into Boomer the kangaroo's pouch and pulled out a hammer. He was kneeling on the deck, trying to fix a broken shutter. "We're not going to leave you two alone here."

"But, Dad, we're fourteen!" Mary-Kate cried. "We haven't had a baby-sitter in, like, weeks!"

"And Katie promised to look after the front desk and keep an eye on us," Ashley added.

"No," Dad said, but Mary-Kate could tell he was weakening. He picked up a nail and started hammering. WHAM! He whacked his thumb. "Ow!" he cried. He dropped the hammer and hopped up and down in pain.

"Honey, it *is* our anniversary," Teri Parker said.

"No. And that's the end of it," Dad grunted, still clutching his sore thumb.

The shutter fell off its hinges and crashed onto his foot.

"Ow!" he yelled, holding his foot. "Well, I suppose a few days off wouldn't hurt...."

The girls saw their parents off the next day. That night was Victoria's yacht party. Mary-Kate spent the day with Katie, trying to learn how to surf. They ended up spending most of the time floating on the surfboards, talking.

"What's his name?" Katie asked, when Mary-Kate told her about the amusement park adventure.

"Pete," Mary-Kate replied. "He's totally cool. But if Victoria ever caught me hanging with him, I'd be history."

Katie lay back on her board. "When I was your age, there was a girl just like Victoria..." she said.

"Really?" Mary-Kate asked.

"There are *always* girls like Victoria. Anyway, I wanted to be in her group so badly. So I stopped doing all the things I liked to do and picked up all the things she liked to do."

"Ooh!" Mary-Kate sat up. "I know this one! You were really miserable because you weren't being true to yourself!"

Katie shook her head. "Actually, I was totally popular and had a blast. But...I was being who *they* wanted me to be. That's no good."

Meanwhile, on the docks, Ashley was getting advice from another source—Shelby.

"Have you ever asked yourself," Ashley began, "what price a girl is supposed to pay for popularity?"

"Yeah," Shelby grunted. "Many times."

Ashley shot a glance at him to see if he was making fun of her. Then she turned her head away quickly. Shelby was gutting a fish. Yuck!

"Follow your heart," Shelby advised her, slicing the fish open. "Be true to yourself," he added, scraping off the scales. "And always use a number-five fishhook. That's the key to happiness."

Fish guts sprayed the deck as Shelby spoke. Ashley backed away. "I'm glad we had this little talk," she murmured. Then she headed for the house. She had a party to get ready for!

Victoria's yacht was even more beautiful than the girls had imagined. It was long, graceful, and white, with colored lights strung from bow to stern.

They were shuttled to the boat in a dinghy. The party had a sixties theme—so Mary-Kate wore her favorite go-go dress. Ashley wore her new necklace with the big, sparkly stone.

Donnie and Ray greeted them as they boarded the yacht. "Come on," Donnie said, grabbing Mary-Kate's hand. "Let's dance."

Donnie and Ray led the girls to the dance floor. Mary-Kate tried to smile politely as she watched Donnie dance. *He must be the worst dancer who ever lived,* she thought as she kept the fake smile plastered to her face.

She glanced across the dance floor to check on Ashley. She could tell Ray really liked Ashley—and it was obvious to her that Ashley could barely stand him. *I'd know that fake smile anywhere,* Mary-Kate thought. She touched her mouth to make sure hers was still in place.

Then she caught sight of Victoria, glaring at Ashley and Ray as she sipped a drink.

Uh-oh, Mary-Kate thought.

A slow song came on. Victoria cut in between Ashley and Ray. "This is *our* song, Ray," she grated. "Remember?"

"No problem," Ashley said quickly. She walked away toward the food table.

Donnie gripped Mary-Kate tightly. He kept moving his face closer and closer to hers. Ugh! Major nacho breath! She kept leaning backward, trying not to breathe. Soon she felt as if she were doing a backbend. *How did I ever think he was cute?* she wondered. *Get me out of this!*

"You're really pretty, Maddie," Donnie said.

"Uh, thanks," Mary-Kate replied. Then she saw his lips begin to pucker.

Oh, no, she thought. *He's going for the kiss! Time for defensive maneuver number forty-one.*

Before his lips could touch hers, Mary-Kate turned her cheek. Donnie's mouth landed awkwardly on the side of her face.

"Um, excuse me," Mary-Kate said, extracting herself from Donnie's grip. "I'm not feeling well."

She hurried across the deck to where Ashley stood alone. "Act like I'm seasick," she told Ashley. "Come on!" Clutching her stomach, she led Ashley down to the lower deck.

"I don't care how popular Donnie is," Mary-Kate told her sister as they leaned against a railing. "He's still a dorko dancer with bad breath. I'd rather hang with Pete and Avery any day of the—"

Her attention was distracted by a commotion at the gangplank. Victoria stood at the entrance to the yacht, trying to block someone's way in.

"This is a closed party," she said.

Two boys dressed in sleek black wet suits pushed their way past her. Pete and Avery! Mary-Kate's heart leaped.

"Invitation only!" Victoria snapped.

"Must've left it in my other wet suit," Avery joked.

"What do you think you're doing here?" Victoria demanded.

"We heard there were some babes aboard," Pete said, looking at Mary-Kate. Victoria shot her a glare.

Donnie stepped forward. "If I ever catch you on our beach again, I'll...I'll..."

"You'll what?" Pete asked. "Finish a sentence?"

Now Ray stepped forward, fists raised. "That's it! We're done talking."

Ray and Donnie moved in on them. Pete and Avery prepared to defend themselves.

"Oh, no!" Ashley gasped.

"Wait!" Victoria stepped between them. "No fighting on Daddy's boat. I've got a better idea."

The boys paused, listening to her.

"A surf war," Victoria suggested. "On Sunday. Winner takes the beach. Loser moves down to Dee Why Beach and never comes back."

It was our first day of high school... all we wanted was to be popular. But we accidentally insulted the most popular girl in school!

We couldn't show our faces anywhere. We thought we were doomed to wear bags over our heads until we graduated! But things changed when we witnessed a robbery on our way home from school.

We had a flock of gangsters after us, so we had to move to Texas and change our names. We would be safe as long as we didn't tell anyone who we really were.

But we just couldn't keep a secret! We had to move again and again. In fact, we moved to so many cities, we almost ran out of places to go!

Finally we had to move to the only place left—
to the other side of the world—Australia!

Moving to Australia was awesome!
We rode in the coolest cars.

We dressed up and went to great parties.

Best of all, we hung out with the cutest boys!

We loved Australia.
We made so many new friends.

We even learned how to ride the waves.

And once the bad guys were sent to jail, everything was perfect! Now it's time to go home, but we'll remember Australia forever!

Mary-Kate and Ashley watched nervously as the boys considered Victoria's idea. Finally, Pete put out his right hand. "Deal," he agreed, shaking Donnie's hand.

Ray and Avery shook on it, too. "All right, everyone," Victoria said. "Back to the party."

Pete and Avery left the boat. Victoria and her friends went to the upper deck to dance. But Mary-Kate and Ashley definitely didn't feel like dancing anymore. They stayed on the lower deck, watching the sunset.

A few minutes later they were startled by someone whistling at the side of the boat. They looked over the rail—and saw Pete and Avery on their Jet Skis.

"Hey, girls!" Pete called. "Want a ride?"

Mary-Kate looked at Ashley. Ashley looked at Mary-Kate. It was as if they could read each other's mind. Smiling, they jumped onto the boys' Jet Skis and rode off into the sunset.

"Whoo-hoo!" Mary-Kate screamed. This was *definitely* the right thing to do!

CHAPTER ELEVEN

"I don't see why we can't tell them the truth," Mary-Kate whispered to Ashley. It was the day after Victoria's party, another beautiful afternoon, and the girls were sitting on a bench near the beach. Pete and Avery were standing in line at a hot dog cart, waiting to buy snacks.

"You mean, tell them we're in Witness Protection?" Ashley whispered back, careful not to let anyone hear. "Oh, they'll love that. 'Hey, want to see a movie? And by the way, we're wanted dead or alive.'"

"We've been here two months already," Mary-Kate said. "Nothing bad has happened. I'm tired of living a lie. I'm tired of being paranoid!"

At that instant, a rough hand clamped down on each of the girls' arms. "Gotcha!" growled a low voice.

The girls spun around. Ashley gasped as she saw who was holding them. Mac and Sidney!

"You goons! I knew you were the bad guys!" Mary-Kate exclaimed.

"Keep your mouths shut, and maybe you'll live to tell about this," Mac threatened.

"That's such an old line," Ashley said, trying to sound brave.

Mac put his face so close to Ashley's, she could smell his stale breath. "We have a license to kill," he said.

"So?" Ashley stared back at him, concentrating on not barfing. "We'll have a learner's permit... soon."

Mac looked confused. Ashley seized her chance. She gave him a hard, swift kick between the legs. Mary-Kate whacked Sidney in the knees.

"Oof!" Sidney groaned.

"Ow!" Mac squealed.

"Run!" Ashley cried. The girls took off down the boardwalk as fast as they could. Up ahead, Pete and Avery were walking toward them, carrying hot dogs.

"Run!" Mary-Kate shouted.

"Why?" Pete asked.

"Look behind you!" said Ashley. She turned and pointed.

The boys looked back. Their eyes widened as they saw Sidney and Mac rushing toward them.

The girls grabbed the boys by the hands and took off, letting the hot dogs fall to the ground.

They ran through the crowds on the boardwalk, hoping to lose the two thugs. Mary-Kate spotted a sign that said PUBLIC TOILET up ahead.

"Quick!" she called. "In there!"

Mary-Kate and Ashley and the two boys ducked into the bathroom. Each took a stall and hid inside, standing on the toilet so no one could see their feet.

Mary-Kate held her breath as she heard Mac and Sidney run panting into the bathroom.

"They've got to be in here somewhere," Mac said. "I saw them run this way."

"You'd better be right," Sidney growled.

Mary-Kate heard their footsteps pacing up and down the bathroom, as if they were trying to decide which stall door to open. At last she heard a *slam* as Sidney pushed open a door.

Mary-Kate peeked over the stall to see whom Sidney had caught.

"Whoa! Sorry, lady!" Sidney grunted. An old cleaning woman had been scrubbing the toilet in that stall. Mary-Kate tried not to laugh as the old woman whacked Sidney with her dirty toilet brush.

"Let's get out of here!" Sidney cried. He and Mac hurried out of the bathroom.

"The coast is clear!" Mary-Kate whispered. They all crept out of the bathroom and peeked around the corner. Mac and Sidney were running down the boardwalk, away from the inn.

"Come on!" Ashley cried, grabbing Avery's hand. She led them all the way back to the Surfside Inn.

The girls paused outside the inn, catching their breath. "Well, thanks for everything, guys," Ashley said.

"Yeah," Mary-Kate put in quickly. "It was a great date. See you."

The girls started up the front steps.

"Uh, girls—" Pete called.

Mary-Kate and Ashley turned around.

"Is there something you want to tell us?" Avery asked.

Uh-oh. "Like?" Mary-Kate prompted.

"Like why you're being chased by two thugs?" Pete said.

"Right," Ashley said. "Excellent question. You want to field that one, Mollie?"

"Maddie," Mary-Kate corrected her sister.

"Listen," she began. She wanted to tell them the truth so badly! "You guys are cool...."

"And we really like you," Ashley continued. "But we're in—"

She paused, looking at Mary-Kate.

"We're in..." Mary-Kate echoed. *Should we tell?*

she wondered. But she already knew the answer. It would be wrong. The more Pete and Avery knew, the more danger *they'd* be in.

"We're in trouble," she said at last.

"But we can't say any more than that," Ashley said.

"Is there anything we can do to help?" Avery asked.

"Right now we kind of have to help ourselves," Ashley told them.

"We'll tell you about it when the time is right, but for now, you'll just have to trust us," Mary-Kate said.

Pete and Avery looked at each other. Then they nodded. "Say no more," Avery said.

"We're working on that skill," Mary-Kate said. They waved good-bye to the boys and went inside the inn.

"Well, I guess we'd better call the FBI—and Mom and Dad," Ashley said with a sigh.

"Are you joking?" Mary-Kate protested. "We can't ask Mom and Dad to move again. And I'm tired of running, too. Come on, Ashley. *We* made this mess." She felt a surge of determination. "We can figure out how to clean it up."

Ashley broke into a grin. "I'm open to that!"

"First, we've got to lose Katie for a few hours." Mary-Kate glanced at Katie, who was busy behind the front desk. The girls approached the desk, not sure how they were going to get rid of Katie.

"Hi, girls," Katie said. "Did you see those mondo waves out there? I can't believe I'm stuck here. I have to finish amortizing the utility allocation for the past twelve years." She sighed and rested her arm on a tall stack of papers.

"We can do that," Mary-Kate offered.

"Really?" Katie's face brightened.

"No sweat," Ashley assured her.

Katie hurried out from behind the front desk. "You guys are awesome!" She waved as she headed outside toward the beach.

"Now what?" Ashley asked.

"We set our trap," Mary-Kate said.

She and Ashley gathered everything they could think of that might help them stop Mac and Sidney. They sprayed hair mousse on the doorknobs. They hoisted a bag of flour to the ceiling, ready to fall on the head of the next person to walk through the front door. They sewed a rug out of banana peels. They scattered glue traps all over the floor and loaded a tennis ball launcher like a cannon, ready to pelt any intruders.

At last Ashley spied Mac and Sidney stalking up the front walk. "They're coming!" she cried.

From a window, the girls watched the thugs approach. "I hope this works," Ashley whispered.

Mac and Sidney walked up the steps and onto the porch. The girls hid under the stairs. Mary-Kate held her breath as she saw the knob on the front door turn slowly.

The door opened. Mac and Sidney stepped inside—right onto the tips of two water skis. The skis flew up and thunked them both in the face. Mac and Sidney collapsed to the floor, out cold.

Mary-Kate and Ashley came out from behind the stairs.

"Huh," Ashley said. "That was easy. Want some lip gloss?"

CHAPTER TWELVE

"Are you going to talk?" Mary-Kate demanded. She was pacing back and forth in front of Mac and Sidney, who were each tied to a surfboard. "I don't want to have to get rough here." She stuck her face close to Mac's. "Tell us why you're after us."

"Never!" Mac cried.

"Okay," Mary-Kate taunted, waving a bottle of nail polish in front of him. "I didn't want to have to do this, but you leave me no choice."

"You wouldn't dare," Mac gasped.

Mary-Kate grinned at Ashley. This was going to be fun.

Before long, Mac's feet were perfectly pedicured, complete with bronze nail polish and smiley faces on the big toes. He wiggled his toes, close to tears.

"Someone's giving us the silent treatment," Ashley said, glaring at Sidney.

Sidney held his lips shut tight.

"Still won't talk, eh? Okay..." Ashley held up a hairbrush and a tube of styling mousse. "Are you looking for a way to go glam one day and natural the next?" she teased.

"You wouldn't dare!" Sidney growled.

Ashley proceeded to style Sidney's hair into an outrageously fluffy hairdo. But Sidney still wouldn't talk.

"They're not cracking," Mary-Kate said to Ashley. "Now what?"

Ashley held up two bikinis.

"Noooo!" screamed Mac and Sidney.

Ashley suddenly heard a phone ring. The sound came from Mac's jacket. She reached into his pocket, grabbed the phone, and clicked it on.

"Hello?" she said in her deepest voice, pretending to be Mac.

Mary-Kate leaned in close to hear.

"Do you idiots have the Kneel Diamond yet?" a man's voice bellowed. With a shock, Ashley recognized the voice. It was Emil Hatchew!

She thought fast. "Please hold," she said in her deep voice. She covered the phone with her hand. "He thinks we have the Kneel Diamond," she whispered to her sister. "Why would he think that?" She toyed with the necklace she had made—the one with the big, sparkly rock.

Mary-Kate's eyes grew perfectly round. She

pointed excitedly to the necklace.

Ashley gasped. "No!"

Mac and Sidney nodded gloomily. "Yes," they said together.

Hatchew's voice screamed through the phone. "Hello! This is a long-distance call!"

Ashley ignored him. She was still trying to take in the incredible truth.

"Wow," she said, touching the stone. "You mean we had it all along? So *that's* why you goons are after us!"

"Bingo," Mac said.

Ashley suddenly knew exactly what to do. She returned to the phone. "Hey, Mr. Hatchew?" she said gleefully. "I hope you won't be mad, but we've got your men tied to surfboards!"

"No!" Sidney cried.

"He's going to kill us!" Mac shouted.

"And the Kneel Diamond sure looks great around my neck," Ashley continued. "Especially with casual wear."

Mac was freaking out. "What are you doing, you blabbermouth?"

"You'll just have to come and get the diamond yourself," Ashley said to Emil Hatchew. "Otherwise, I'm going to go *Titanic* on you and throw it into the ocean. Have a nice trip. Oh, and I recommend Qantas. It's a long flight."

She hung up the phone. Mac and Sidney were shaking so hard, the surfboards rattled against the floor.

Mary-Kate was staring at her sister in shock. "I assume you've got a plan," she said.

"Uh...sort of," Ashley replied. Now that she'd started the ball rolling, she suddenly felt totally nervous.

"Untie us, girls!" Mac begged. "We've got to get out of here before Hatchew gets us."

"Otherwise, he'll put our bums on the barbie and have us for brekkie," Sidney said. He paused, looking surprised. "I have no idea where that came from."

"Okay," Ashley agreed, untying Sidney. "If you promise not to bother us anymore."

"Don't worry," Mac promised.

Mary-Kate loosened Mac's ropes. "Sure you guys don't want to stick around and help us stop Hatchew?"

"You mean go straight?" Sidney asked, rubbing his wrists. "Turn to the side of good, away from the darkness of evil?" He paused, staring dreamily into the distance. "Can you imagine a day in which I escort little old ladies across the street, help abandoned puppies find new homes, and work for the good of all humankind?"

"Uh, no," Mac said after an awkward pause.

Sidney sighed. "Me, either."

Once Mac and Sidney were gone, Ashley and Mary-Kate went to their room. Boomer the kangaroo was sitting in a chair in front of the TV.

"I beeped Agent Banner," Ashley announced. "The FBI should be here by tomorrow morning."

"Tomorrow's the surf war. Surfies against Victoria's posse," Mary-Kate reminded her. She bit her lip. "I hope the FBI shows up before Hatchew."

"It's all under control," Ashley assured her. "The FBI catches Hatchew trying to make off with the diamond. He goes to jail. And we all go home. Simple!"

Mary-Kate sighed. "I hope so."

CHAPTER THIRTEEN

The next day Manley Beach buzzed with excitement. Crowds of kids gathered to watch the surf wars. The surfers were busy waxing their boards while three judges set up a scoring table.

Mary-Kate and Ashley arrived with Pete and Avery, who were going to compete. Ashley spotted Sheila and Leonard walking near the water, holding hands.

"Sheila! Lenny!" she called, running up to them. "Wait up!"

Sheila and Lenny stopped and turned around. "I want to apologize to you," Ashley said. "For blabbing. What I did was awful. I hope you can forgive me—and we can be friends."

Sheila smiled. "Ah, that's okay, Abby. You forced me and Lenny to openly declare our love for each other. We're getting married."

Ashley's jaw dropped. "What!"

Sheila and Lenny laughed. "Just joking!" Sheila said. "You Yanks are so gullible." She leaned closer to Ashley and added, "Look at Victoria and her posse over there. I hope the surfies stick it to them."

Ashley listened to the pep talk Victoria was giving her surfers. "Go get those surfies!" she cried. "Barro those bignotes! Blot out those boofheads! Destroy those drongos! Let's win this thing, shall we?"

Then a judge blew a whistle, and the surf wars began. Ashley ran across the beach to join Mary-Kate and the surfie crowd.

Ray surfed first. He ran out into the ocean and immediately caught a huge wave. He surfed it perfectly. Even Ashley had to admit he was very good.

The judges gave him a nine out of ten.

Next went Pete. "Go, Pete!" Mary-Kate shouted as he rode a beautiful curl. The judges gave him a nine, too.

Next Donnie surfed, then Avery. They both did well, receiving scores of eight each. As the surfers from the two teams alternated, the judges posted their scores on a board. The surfies had only one surfer left—Jake Goolaging. And he needed a perfect ten if the surfies were going to win.

Jake dropped his board and cried out, "Ow! Me widgie! Me widgie got bent!"

He clutched his hand. He had hurt his finger when he had grabbed his board.

"What are we going to do, Pete?" Avery asked. "The bloke can't surf in that condition."

There was a long pause. Then Avery and Pete both turned to stare at Ashley.

Oh, no, she thought. *Do they want me to do what I think they want me to do?*

"Me?" she cried. "Surf in a contest?" Her heart pounded nervously. What if she made them lose?

"It's not about winning, Ashley," Avery said. "It's about trying."

"Go for it, Agnes!" Mary-Kate cheered.

"Abby!" Ashley corrected her sister.

"Whatever!" all the surfies said.

Ashley took a deep breath—and grabbed a surfboard. Out on the water, a nice medium-size wave came. Ashley paddled…and jumped up on her board.

"Hooray!" the crowd cheered.

Ashley felt a little wobbly, but she managed to stay on the board and make it to shore. Mary-Kate ran to hug her. The surfies cheered wildly for her.

All eyes turned to the judges. They held up their scorecard.

Six!

Ashley groaned. She'd blown it! The surfies had lost. That meant Victoria's posse had gained control of the beach forever.

"We won! We won, we won!" Victoria shouted, jumping up and down.

"I'm sorry we lost," Ashley said to Avery.

Avery threw his arm around her shoulders. "Forget the contest—you were awesome out there! Dee Why Beach has some good waves, anyway."

He is so cool! Ashley thought happily.

"Come on, mates!" Pete called. "We're heading over to Dee Why Beach. Who's coming?"

Mary-Kate, Ashley, Pete, and Avery led the way. As they walked, Mary-Kate glanced back. She was startled to see *all* the kids following them down the beach. Not just the surfies. Not just the nerds. Even the kids from Victoria's posse were with them!

Mary-Kate caught sight of Victoria. She was standing alone on Manley Beach.

"Wait!" Victoria called. "I won! This is my beach. I won this beach!"

The rest of the kids ignored her. But Mary-Kate couldn't help feeling sorry for her. She ran back to where Victoria stood, claiming her territory.

"Come on!" Mary-Kate called, smiling and waving Victoria toward her.

Victoria looked around and saw that no one had stayed to celebrate with her. With a shrug, she ran toward Mary-Kate.

"Well," Mary-Kate said when she joined Ashley at the beach party. She stood back and watched a couple of kids tossing a boomerang around. "I think things have worked out pretty well. All the loose ends have been tied up. All the *t*'s have been crossed, all the *i*'s have been dotted, the cake is out of the oven, and Grandma is putting on the icing—"

Ashley tapped her on the shoulder. "Uh, I think you forgot about something," she murmured. She pointed over Mary-Kate's shoulder.

Mary-Kate turned to look.

Whoops. She'd forgotten all about Emil Hatchew! But there he was—right behind her!

Hatchew and two big, mean-looking henchmen took a step toward the girls. "So," he growled in his low, evil voice, "we finally meet again, girls."

CHAPTER FOURTEEN

"I believe you have something that belongs to me," Hatchew said, eyeing the diamond Ashley wore.

The other kids stood in a half-circle behind the girls, staring. Mary-Kate stepped between Hatchew and Ashley. "Not so fast, Hatchew," she warned.

"Bless you!" everyone on the beach shouted. Hatchew scowled at them.

"Okay!" Ashley called out. "FBI guys, you can come out now!"

Mary-Kate and Ashley looked around for help to appear.

But no one came!

I beeped them, Ashley thought in frustration. *What's taking them so long?*

"Agent Banner?" she called. "Agent Norm?" She paused, hoping one of them would jump out of the bushes or something. But nothing happened. "Agent anyone?" she added in a small voice.

"Great plan," Mary-Kate grumbled.

"Let's keep this brief." Hatchew yanked the diamond necklace from Ashley's neck. Behind him, a seaplane swooped in, landing in the water.

"My ride is here," Hatchew said. He snapped his fingers at his henchmen. "Turn them into shark bait," he ordered, pointing to the girls. Then he calmly walked to the shoreline and jumped into a waiting dinghy. The dinghy zipped off toward the seaplane.

The two henchmen began to advance on Mary-Kate and Ashley. The girls backed up nervously. *How are we ever going to get out of this?* Ashley wondered.

Then Pete and Avery jumped in front of the girls. "If you want them, you've got to go through us," Pete said. "Right, Avery?"

"Right!" Avery called.

Ashley bit her lip. She appreciated the gesture— but she didn't want to see Avery and Pete get creamed!

The two goons stepped forward threateningly. Pete and Avery took a step backward. So did Mary-Kate and Ashley.

The four of them kept backing up as Hatchew's henchmen closed in on them.

Then someone called, "Hey! Pick on someone your own size!"

That voice! Mary-Kate thought. *That sounded just like Sidney!*

She whirled around to see Mac and Sidney standing behind her.

"What are you guys doing here?" she asked.

"We were wondering if you could touch up our nails," Mac replied. He winked at her. Then he stepped forward and punched one of the goons in the jaw. The man tumbled onto the sand.

"See, I just chipped one," Mac added, glancing at his hand.

"Look!" Ashley cried, pointing toward the ocean. "Hatchew is getting away!"

Hatchew's dinghy had reached the seaplane. Hatchew was just getting ready to step aboard. Then Mary-Kate grabbed the boomerang from one of the kids who'd been tossing it. She heaved the boomerang at Hatchew. It flew across the beach and hit Hatchew with a *whack*, knocking him into the water.

Ashley patted her sister on the back. "Nice shot!"

Hatchew struggled in the water as the tide washed him back to shore. Suddenly, Katie ran up in her bathing suit.

"Good work, girls," she said to Mary-Kate and Ashley. "Come on—let's go get him." She ran toward the shoreline.

Mary-Kate and Ashley looked at each other, confused. What was Katie doing there? They shrugged and ran after her.

Emil Hatchew lay exhausted on the sand, soaking wet. "Emil Hatchew," Katie said. "You're under arrest." She produced a silver badge.

"What?" Mary-Kate and Ashley cried together.

Katie grinned at the girls. "Agent Katie Smith—FBI. At your service." She somehow pulled a pair of handcuffs from her bikini and slapped them on Hatchew.

"FBI?" Mary-Kate echoed. Her head was reeling with all this new information. She'd thought Katie was a surfing instructor!

"We thought you girls might need some extra care," Katie explained. "I was assigned to watch you two and wait for Hatchew to make his move on the diamond."

She took the diamond from around Hatchew's neck. "You're going behind bars for life, Mr. Hatchew—where you belong."

"All right," Mary-Kate said. "*Now* things are really tied up. Am I right, Ashley?"

Ashley nodded happily. "Mom and Dad will be psyched to go home. Mac and Sidney will get a piece of the reward money for helping recover the Kneel Diamond—"

"Look!" Mary-Kate interrupted. "Victoria is apologizing to the Sheilas for being so mean to them."

Victoria stood humbly in front of a line of Sheilas. "Sorry, Sheila," she said. "Sorry, Sheila. Sorry, Sheila. Sorry, Sheila..."

Ashley laughed. Pete and Avery ran up to the girls and took their hands.

"Here's the best part," Mary-Kate added as she bopped to the music. "We get to dance with the coolest guys in Sydney!"

Ashley grinned. "And that's fair dinkum!"

Can Mary-Kate and Ashley Keep a Secret?
Find out in their NEW movie

Mary-Kate Olsen   **Ashley Olsen**

Our Lips Are Sealed

Filmed in Sydney, Australia

DUALSTAR
VIDEO

MAKE YOUR OWN MOVIE MAGIC™
WITH THE
MARY-KATE AND ASHLEY
CELEBRITY PREMIERE FASHION DOLLS

AVAILABLE
MARCH 200

Go behind the scenes
Mary-Kate gets ready

...and Ashley sets
the scene.

DUALSTAR
CONSUMER PRODUCTS

outta-site!
mary-kateandashley.com

mary-kateandashley

MATTEL

outta site!

mary-kateandashley.com

Register Now

Check out
"Now Read This" on
mary-kateandashley.com
for an exclusive
online chapter preview
of our upcoming book!

DUALSTAR
ONLINE